Title and Subtitle

Title: Love from Another Planet
Subtitle: Alien Romance Short Story

Copyright

From the Author:
Thank you for purchasing this book.

Table of Contents

Love from Another Planet
Description

He is tall, toned, and has long black hair that he keeps in a braid. Every woman's wet dream. His name is Jake. The guy next door that Mel is almost obsessed with. Scratch that. Mel *is* obsessed with Jake. They have been neighbors for some months now, and Jake hasn't ever looked her way to say more than a greeting.

No amount of short skirts and cleavage-revealing tops she wears whenever she wants to talk to him makes him blink.

Mel is a man-whore, a fierce go-getter raised by a mom who is embittered with life. Mel didn't know how to take no, and she wants to get into Jake's pants, by any means possible. As long as he is a man, she is a strong believer that her seduction skills will have him where she wants.

The only thing she didn't see coming, is that Jake is *not* a man.

Chapter 1

Mel rushed out of her office building and to her car. As she unlocked the Jeep Cherokee, she prayed the road leading to her neighborhood was still accessible. She glanced around her and chided herself for waiting so long to leave the office. It was Friday and on Fridays, she could leave any time after two o'clock in the afternoon. She checked the time on her dashboard. It was a quarter past three. Looking at the blanket of snow around her, she hoped the decision to stay back and sort out some paperwork wasn't one she would come to regret.

Snow season had started just that morning and the downpour had been relentless. Mel took off her jacket as she settled in the driver's seat, shivering exaggeratedly as she turned on the heat. She stared at her exposed thighs, wondering what motivated her to pick one of her shortest skirts as her outfit for one of the coldest days so far in the year. She shook her legs vigorously, trying to get some life in them, and said a small prayer as she turned the key in the ignition, grinning in relief when it started on the first try. It was starting to give her a few troubles here and there, but in her usual careless manner, she had continued to forget to get it checked out.

"Tomorrow," she lied to herself for the umpteenth time.

Mel had a love-hate relationship with snow. On the one hand, she loved playing in the snow and did so with reckless abandon. It was the one thing that guaranteed the appearance of her innermost child. On the other hand, she absolutely hated having to shovel snow off her doorstep each morning and always suspected, one of these days, she would slip and break her neck, considering her obsession with stilettos. She was also really bad at driving in these conditions and usually gripped her steering until her knuckles turned white. She reminded herself of the new snow tires she had installed just a week ago, but this did nothing to ease her fears.

Although Michigan was only the tenth snowiest state in the country, Grand Rapids was one of the snowiest cities and its snow patterns could be highly unpredictable. One minute, you could be walking on dry ground, an hour later, you and your car would be stuck. As Mel approached her neighborhood, keeping her speed to 40 mph and under, she noticed that Jake had fallen victim to the “Rapids snow trap,” as she liked to call it. She slowed her car to a stop and studied him like she always did. Tall and deliciously toned, he moved like a man who was always sure of himself, always certain of his next move. At that moment, he was bent over, checking his right rear tire and offering Mel an excellent view of his taut backside.

"Ooh yum," she purred lustfully. Her breath caught in her throat as he stood upright, flipping his thick, long braid of black hair. She had never wanted a man more. He was a tall drink of water and she wanted, not just a sip, but the entire glass.

Mel grinned, knowing this was another opportunity to get close to this elusive man. Jake and she had been neighbors for months and there was almost nothing she hadn't done to try and get his attention. Tiny skirts, cleavage-revealing tops, tiny dresses, flirty tones, and looks. Nothing had worked. Zero. Zilch.

"Here we go again," she whispered to herself as she put the car into gear and drove the few yards that separated them.

As Mel stopped beside his Charger, Jake turned around and frowned. She stepped out of her car, hoping that frown was as a result of the obvious car trouble he was having and not due to her presence. She inspected the scene, noticed the skid marks just before where her car was now parked, and realized what must have happened. His car must have skidded off the road and into one of the heaps of snow left on either side of the road when the plow must have run through earlier.

"Hey there," she said, offering him the most flirtatious smile she could muster. "Everything okay?"

"Car trouble," Jake responded coldly and turned around glaring at the Dodge with obvious anger. Mel found his anger funny but decided this wasn't a very good time to laugh.

"Hey," she tried again, touching his arm affectionately to better keep his attention this time. "It's getting really cold out here. Let me give you a lift home."

"It's a mere twenty-minute walk. I'll be fine, thank you." He stared at her hand on his upper arm as if confused as to how it had gotten there.

Mel noticed his stare but was unfazed. "You're not thinking this through, Jake. It's really coming down now. Your hair is turning white."

Jake ran his gloves hand through his hair, seemingly self-conscious for the first time she could remember. The man was human after all. She laughed, tugging his hand. "Come on."

"All right," he responded gruffly, "let me lock up." She grinned victoriously and skipped to her car.

Jake watched her skip away and shook his head, wondering how she didn't trip and break her neck in those heels. The woman's spirit was incorrigible and, no matter how cold he was, her attitude toward him remained cheerful and flirtatious. Highly flirtatious. She was stunning; a fact she obviously was aware of and used to her advantage to get whatever she wanted. He was on her radar and she wasn't ashamed to show it.

There were times Jake regretted his coldness toward her, but it was imperative he kept his distance from people for reasons they could never know about. He wondered if she genuinely wanted him or if she was just fascinated as people usually were with things that seemed to be out of reach. He wondered if she would still be interested if she knew just who he was. What he was. He chuckled, picturing her reaction.

Jake consciously stopped his wandering thoughts, reminding himself he was here for more important reasons than what currently occupied his mind. He called the car club, gave the operator his coordinates from his car's GPS, and hung up. They had promised him a one-hour pick-up. He looked at the sky, then around him doubting they'd be able to keep to their word, but hoping all the same. He got his wallet from his glove compartment, took out his jacket from the backseat, and locked the car with a push of a button on his key. Resigned to at least five minutes of flirtatious torture from Mel, he opened the door and settled in the passenger seat.

"Thank you for assisting me," he said gruffly, trying his darndest not to stare at her exposed, creamy thighs. How she was able to put that on in this weather amazed him.

"You're welcome," Mel responded with one of her lightning grins. She noticed the direction of his glance and, for the first time that day, putting on this skirt didn't seem like such a stupid move.

"You know, having snow tires would have saved you from that mess. Roads get pretty slippery this time of the year," she admonished.

"You don't say," Jake replied wryly. He was aware he had been foolish and hated being reminded of his foolishness. This wasn't his first snow, after all. He had been so engrossed in work, he had begun to forget basic things he should do.

Mel studied him, noticing the discomfort he was trying to hide. She thought back trying to recall the last person who had been in her passenger seat. She gave up, unable to remember who it was. No matter, whoever it had been, they certainly didn't possess the length of legs he did. She pictured those legs devoid of the jeans they were currently enclosed in and entwined with hers. The thought sent shivers down her spine.

Jake could stand the discomfort no further and found the lever to the side, pulling on it and creating more legroom.

"I'll return that to its former position once I step out," he stated matter-of-factly, not even glancing at her.

"Let it stay that way. With those tires, you'll probably be needing a lift from me a few more times in the coming days." She grinned at him and could swear a hint of a smile appeared at the edge of his lips. Yup, she thought victoriously, there was definitely a twitch somewhere there.

"I assure you, Ms. Adams," he drawled, "this situation won't be repeated anytime soon." He gestured as he spoke, and she couldn't help but stare at his arms. The denim he wore was folded to the elbows, affording her a delicious view of thickly veined forearms that looked capable of smashing through walls at a first attempt. She wondered briefly, what it would feel like to have those arms encircle her. Lift her off her feet...

Mel hated being referred to as "Ms. Adams." but on the tongue of this man, she could feel her insides melt. *Oh, great*, she thought, feeling the familiar warmth spring forth at her center. She wanted, no, needed this man in her bed. As soon as possible. And she was ready to do whatever it took to get him there.

So far, she couldn't remember any man she wanted successfully resisting her. That record wasn't about to be spoiled. Especially not by the one she was hottest for. She smiled as her confidence rose. She had been able to get a hint of a smile from him. She considered that progress and decided it could only get better from here out.

As Mel turned onto the street they both shared with four other neighbors, she felt bad the trip was coming to an end. This was the most fun she had had in a while and she had tried all she could to stretch it out, reducing her speed to an agonizingly slow 25 miles per hour.

Jake had looked at her at some point and asked, "Do you always drive like this?"

"Like how?" she had asked, feigning innocence.

"Like a ninety-year-old woman," he responded.

Mel had laughed at that. "Just being careful. You know how the roads get at this time." In fact, she didn't want this trip to end and was just starting to wonder if there wasn't a way she could offer him an alternative destination.

She stopped just before his one-story house and Jake turned to face her, reaching for the latch simultaneously.

"I appreciate your kind gesture and hope to reward you in kind soon."

"Ohhh," Mel responded flirtatiously, "I have quite a few ideas on how you can reward me. Immediately actually."

Jake actually smiled this time and Mel's heart melted. *Damn, this man is fine.*

"Thank you, Mel," he responded and moved to exit the Jeep. Now, Mel was starting to panic, knowing she didn't want him away from her side anytime soon.

"Hold on, Jake," she blurted. "I've got a big dinner in the fridge and no one to share it with. I could heat it up and get it ready in five. Join me?"

He paused, seemingly considering the offer and Mel held her breath. He had never even given a hint of considering any offers she had made in the past. Her mind raced with possibilities but she was dragged back to earth when he responded, "Some other time, Mel. Lots of work to do."

"All right," she responded, faking a smile as she watched Jake get out of her car, shut the door, and walk to his front door without so much as a backward glance. She was unable to drive off and stayed right where she was with her heart racing. She had had desires before. Several times. And being a woman who went for what she wanted, she often fulfilled these desires. With this man, however, it was beyond desire. He only had to look at her and her knees would be a little more than useless. She ached for him and found herself peeking through windows hoping for just the sight of him. What was wrong with her? She had touched herself over the months, imagining it was him touching her, but that was no longer enough. She wanted the real deal.

She looked at where he had sat for the past ten minutes and, before thinking about it, leaned in to sniff the leather seat. As she took a deep breath in, the smell of him punched through her body and she groaned audibly, unable to resist the dull ache that had started at her center and spread all through her. It was a smell unlike any she had ever encountered, and it confused and aroused her in equal, intense measures.

As Mel settled into her driveway, she finally admitted that what she had for Jake was beyond desire. It was beyond craving and longing. It was an obsession. Pure, unadulterated obsession.

Chapter 2

Mel was restless. More restless than she could ever remember. She had done everything she could think of to relax. Lit her scented candles. Played her Enya playlist on her surround sound home theater. Even downed a glass of red wine. Nothing worked. What used to calm her nerves seemed to all be working in the exact opposite direction of what she wanted. Mel felt ganged up on.

Jake was on her mind and she couldn't pull him out. The man was a mystery. He hardly ever spoke, hardly ever smiled and his face was a blank expressionless slate most of the time. It was like nothing got to him.

Mel remembered the first day she had noticed him. He was already in the neighborhood when she moved in three months ago. She had moved from Manhattan on a whim; a spontaneous decision she never really thought through. That was who Mel was—a woman who got an idea, spent only three seconds thinking about it and chased after it. She was as adventurous as anyone could possibly get. Sometimes too adventurous, she admitted to herself, remembering a few times she had been burned by her decision-making. Nonetheless, Mel was a woman who knew she had just one life and lived it to the fullest.

She had been settled in for a solid week before she realized she was yet to meet anyone in the immaculately groomed house right next to hers. She studied it, noting the metal picket fence about four feet high and with pointed tops. The garden surrounding the front of the house was lush and obviously well-taken care of. Mel didn't know much about flowers, but even her untrained eye could see the numerous species on display, all blooming and perfectly trimmed. Her curiosity increased as she wondered how a person who managed to keep this place in such immaculate shape could escape her view for an entire week. The windows were not boarded up, but they could have as well been for the thick curtains that were always firmly in place and never moved an inch. Did the occupant have an ongoing beef with fresh air?

After two more days of not seeing her next-door neighbor, Mel could hold in her curiosity no longer and marched to the front door of the house directly across from hers. The knock was answered by a shy, smiling face. Mary. Mary had been the first one to welcome Mel to the neighborhood, offering her homemade chocolate chip cookies and a cheap bottle of red wine. Mel observed her like she always did, agreeing with herself again that no other name asides Mary would have fit Mary. It was hard to explain. She was just a Mary.

"Hey, girl!" Mel declared cheerfully. "Time to live a little."

Mary's brows rose as she noticed the bottle of wine in Mel's hands. She wasn't surprised. Matter of fact, she had seen this coming from the first day she had met Mel. She had sensed this woman would be a delightful distraction. She was delighted she wasn't wrong. She needed the distraction.

"It's just..." Mary glanced back into the house and at the old grandfather clock in the hallway, "three o'clock. Quite early, wouldn't you say?" she asked, smiling shyly and twirling the gold chain on her neck.

"I won't tell if you don't," Mel responded, winking at her. "Come on, just girl talk with your new favorite neighbor. What could it hurt?"

Mary smiled as she let her new neighbor in. What could it hurt indeed? Mel had proceeded to engage Mary in some premium girl talk, regaling her with tales of the New York life and trying to get her to open up to her as well. The wine certainly seemed to work as, after a few sips, Shy Mary turned out to be quite the talker. Mel danced around a few topics before finally settling on the real reason she had come.

"Hey," she started. "First day we talked, you assured me there was a beau on the horizon. Right next to me in fact. 'Hot guy' were your words."

Mary giggled, feeling the wine "My words were, a 'highly attractive young man."

"*Potato* potato," Mel responded. "Same thing. It's been almost ten days and I haven't seen anybody. What gives?"

"He's a really private guy. Very difficult to see. Near impossible to tell if he's home or not. I've seen him shake Michael's hand twice and we've said hello once. That's been it."

Michael was Mary's husband and was a manager at one of the banks in the area. Mel couldn't remember which. As if on cue, there was the sound of the front door opening. Mary's eyes are round as saucers as she glanced at the clock and realized they had been at it for over 2 hours.

***

The first time Mel had seen him was a memory she would never forget. She couldn't sleep and decided to step out to her porch and onto her swing set that was starting to become her favorite place. She had taken no more than three steps out the front door when she noticed a figure on the porch of the house next to hers. He was tall, pale and the moon highlighted the long, thick braid of hair going down his back. His head was tilted, staring at the sky with such intensity she tried to trace his gaze, wondering what must be up there. Her breath caught as she realized this must be her evasive neighbor. She watched him for what felt like forever, wondering how a person could be so still and unmoving for so long. She was starting to wonder if her mind had, in her tired state, conjured a statue of an ancient Indian chief when he turned sharply and walked back into the house. He had not seen her. Either that or he just didn't consider it important to initiate any dialogue with her.

Mel saw him a few more times after that, guessing correctly that his stare-at-the-sky routine was a regular one. The more she stared at him in the half-darkness, the more she felt drawn to him. She gathered boldness and eventually would try to kick off conversations with him, all of which failed. He was never actually rude, he just seemed very distant and disinterested. She tried flirting and that failed as well. For the first time in her life, there was a man who wasn't distracted by her body, who didn't look at her with lust. She hated it. There was a silent strength about him, something in his gaze that suggested great knowledge and something about his general carriage that threatened to drive Mel mad with curiosity. Who was this man? What was his story?

Mel peeped out the curtain as she heard a sound. She sees what must be the car club guy returning Jake's car. She stared as they had a brief conversation, nodding in the direction of his Dodge. There was a moment of silence where Jake seemed to ponder on a decision, after which he signed a pad and nodded his thanks. Mel expected him to turn around and head back home, but he surprised her, driving directly behind the tow truck. Maybe he was going to get those snow tires installed, Mel thought. Good decision.

Then it hit her, she wouldn't get a better chance than now to find some answers about this mystery man. Michael and Mary had gone on a delayed honeymoon, the house facing Jake's was up for sale and the other neighbors were too far out to notice a thing. Mel accessed herself, gauging to be sure every part of her mind understood what she was about to do and approved of it.

She bit her lip nervously as she approached her front door. Pausing at the door, she wondered just what she was doing and what she hoped to achieve from it. Common sense seemed to gain ground for a few seconds, but curiosity eventually emerged victorious. As nervous as she was, she knew herself and knew that she had already come to a decision. She would go through Jake's house. She would find her answers.

Chapter 3

Mel stepped out of her house and looked down the street; first in the direction she had last seen Jake, then in the opposite direction. Quiet. Just like she expected. It was one of the reasons she had splurged her life's savings to buy this house. Mel was the life of every party, outspoken and outgoing—a social butterfly. However, when all of that was done with, Mel needed her space and quiet and would almost lose her mind if she didn't find a way to get it. It was almost like she had two personalities. Failing to really understand them, she simply chose to embrace both sides.

She walked casually and was soon in Jake's yard. She casually unbolted the gate which seemed more like a marker than for actual protection. As Mel approached the door, she wondered what she would do if it were to be locked. She didn't exactly have the skill set required to pick a lock, and even if she did, she seriously doubt she would put it to use. As she twisted the knob, she once again wondered just what it was she was doing. Pushing the thought aside, she twisted it all the way, delighted to discover the door was unlocked. She quickly stepped in and shut the door behind her.

Taking a deep breath, Mel turned around and began her forbidden tour. Just like all the houses on this street, the door led to a short hallway and Mel could see a coat hanger just to the side. She got to the end of the hallway and was greeted by a large semi-circle of living room space. To the one side was a kitchen space that was so pristine she could swear he had never used it. To the other side was a stairwell she assumed led to the master bedroom. She was saving that for last.

Jake had obviously done quite a lot of work here, as, unlike the other houses, there were no dividing walls in sight.

She loved the loft-style arrangement he had achieved. She noted the absence of pictures and any other personal items one would expect to see in inhabited space. She thought it looked more like a four-star hotel room than a home. *So far so good,* she thought, a tad disappointed, nothing out of the ordinary. Nothing informative.

Mel considered rummaging through the kitchen drawers but reminded herself she had limited time and decided that, if she wanted to discover intimate details about this man, the bedroom was where she needed to be. Mel took a step in that direction, then paused as she heard a beep. It was subtle, and if the neighborhood weren't so quiet, chances were, she would have missed it. She paused, holding her breath and listening to be sure. It came again—a beep then another sound she couldn't quite identify. Mel traced the sound, walking toward a row of sculptures she had noticed earlier but didn't want to take the time to inspect. Now, she looked closer, realizing that the sculptures were of creatures she couldn't recognize, all placed against a wall painted in tiny black and white squares like a chessboard. As she approached, she noticed each creature had glowing red eyes that seemed to brighten and fade in unison. Mel gulped, the first hint of intense anxiety starting to come on her. She pushed away from the fear and soldiered on. She squeezed between two of the scary sculptures and pressed her left ear against the wall. The beeping and the strange sound were suddenly magnified, although, still faint. There was something beyond that wall.

As Mel frantically moved her palms across the wall, searching for a latch or lever, her conscience screamed at her that this was a severe invasion of privacy. Mel justified her actions, convincing herself that if there was something sinister going on in the house next to hers, she deserved to know. He could be a terrorist for all she knew. Mel turned around, frustrated.

Her eyes narrowed as she took another look at the weird sculpted creatures. She stooped and started a body inspection of each one, not exactly sure what it was she was supposed to look out for but knowing she had to access that room beyond the wall. As she ran her hands across the sculptures, she marveled at the smoothness, wondering what material was used. She had done a six-month sculpting course in Marseilles, during her gap year and she had seen and touched some of the most exquisite pieces known to mankind. They all, however, paled in comparison to what she was currently touching. The sculpture she was currently touching looked like what the result of a mating session of a hawk and a wild boar would be. *The beast, if it existed, would be a powerful one*, Mel thought, caressing the powerful muscles in wonder. She looked up into the glaring eyes of the creature and for the first time, noticed it had a horn protruding from its nose region. She frowned, squinting as she noticed what seemed like a demarcating line between the protruding horn and the rest of the face. It almost seemed detachable. Skeptical, she slowly reached out and grabbed the horn, heart in her mouth as she gently pulled. The lever responded easily to her pull and, soundlessly, the checkered wall swung inward, exposing a dimly lit room. Mel took two steps in and paused in her tracks. She couldn't believe the view before her.

The first thing she noticed was the screens. Lots and lots of screens in varying sizes and shapes. The screens formed a huge semi-circle facing a wide swivel armchair. The permanent dent in the leather seat was proof that a person sat in it often. Mel felt the hair on the back of her neck stand upright as she saw the content on the screens. To the right were four screens displaying a quick sequence of what she could only deduce were numbers. She could only deduce because these characters were ones she had never seen before. The computers seemed to be carrying out some complicated calculations non-stop, beeping when what seemed like a solution had been found every few seconds. She had found the source of the beep and she was even more confused than before this room was revealed to her. To the left were three screens—one displaying what seemed like stats also in a language she couldn't make any sense of, the other displaying a gallery of what seemed like the different phases of human existence, and the third, a confusing jumble of pictures and numbers Mel didn't even try to make sense of.

Front and center was a huge, fifty-inch screen showing what seemed like MRI scans of some sort of the human body. This screen seemed paused and displayed no movement. Mel's head was spinning. She had never been more confused. She turned around, slowly assessing the rest of the room. Her eye caught something in the corner, what seemed like a pot of sorts. There was a soft, gurgling sound coming from there and she recognized it as the second sound she had heard earlier. She walked cautiously to it and discovered a blue thick liquid, gurgling gently as though it were boiling. She noticed that this pot of liquid was connected to glass hoses leading to a black, shiny box at the center of the room. Protruding out of the box were smaller glass hoses connected to all the screens above it. For the first time, Mel noticed that, even with the paraphernalia of gadgets contained in the room, there wasn't a single wire or chord. Her eyes traveled back and forth, assessing the connection and trying to understand it. She concluded that the pot of gurgling liquid must be the power source.

Mel had seen enough. She was light-headed and was starting to sway. She couldn't make sense of anything she had seen and, rushing out of the room, she pulled the protruding horn once more, shutting the compartment. She rushed to the front door, ready to leave, but paused, hand on the knob. She had gone this far, she would as well find out everything she needed to. She rubbed her sweaty hands on her sweater, noting the goosebumps on her thighs.

Back in the room, Mel was staring at what was supposed to be a wardrobe but looked more like a portal. A blue circle of light akin to the one downstairs glowed, encircled by a square metal frame with strange markings. Even as she thought of it, she felt silly. This wasn't a sci-fi Hollywood movie. Portals didn't exist. “So, what is it you're looking at?” a voice mocked.

Struggling to swallow, Mel slowly reached out, fighting every instinct screaming at her. She was just going to put in one arm, see what happened.

Just before she reached the blue light, she heard the front door slam. *Shit! Jake was home.* She turned around frantically, needing an out or at least a place to hide. Her mind threw a million suggestions at her, and as she glanced at the wardrobe area again, she realized it had transformed into just that—a wardrobe. Without thinking, she dived inside, crawling to the farthest corner and pushing forward the clothes she didn't notice before. She held her breath, hoping that, by some miracle, she would leave this place she had no business being in undetected.

The bedroom door swung open and she could see through the crack in the door how he paused, looking about with a slight from on his face. "God, please," she prayed in her heart. She watched, barely breathing as he stripped, taking off every stitch of clothing and flinging them on the bed. Forgetting the current situation, Mel was temporarily aroused, watching the naked flesh of this man she had desired for so long. He seemed in a foul mood. *Great,* Mel thought. *Just great.*

Suddenly, Jake transformed. Her mind struggled to comprehend what she was seeing. The man was changing. His skin had become a translucent blue, his jaw extended to a sharp point, he had grown to at least seven feet and she thought she couldn't tell how many there were, she was certain his toes totaled more than ten. Unable to hold back any longer, Mel let out a short cry of panic, putting her hands over her mouth immediately she realized what she had done. It was too late. He had heard. As the creature that was once Jake walked toward her hiding place, Mel screamed louder than she ever had. Before she passed out, she remembered seeing yellow, snake-like eyes staring down at her and wondering if this was the end.

Chapter 4

The world was a blur as Mel's eyes opened. She blinked slowly, trying to recollect where she was and what had happened. She shook her head, trying to clear it and opened her eyes again, actually seeing for the first time. Jake was seated in front of her, his arms rested on his knees as he leaned toward her, staring at her blankly. He was again the Jake she knew, human and without ten toes. For a minute, Mel wondered if she had dreamed it all. If she had been so afraid of being caught she had conjured up an image in her mind.

Looking at him, she didn't think so. She was beginning to tremble with fear again. *What the fuck are you?!* her mind screamed, but the words just wouldn't form.

"What are you doing in my house, Melanie?" Jake asked quietly, breaking the silence. *How had he known her full name?* She wondered. She had never shared it with anyone else apart from family. Mel locked her lips and tried to shift in her chair. That was when she realized she had been tied up. Her eyes rounded in fear and she could feel panic starting to set in. She locked her lips nervously and forcefully swallowed the lump in her throat.

"Why am I tied up, Jake?" she asked, hating the tremble in her voice.

He said nothing In response to this, he just stared at her.

Jake stared at the human female, mad at himself. He had become so used to the calmness and serenity this place offered, he had become sloppy. What was to remain secret had been exposed. He chewed his lower lip, doing some fast thinking as to how he was going to handle this situation. She was terrified, he noted, noticing her darting eyes and shallow breathing. If he was to contain this situation, he had to first, calm her down.

"Deep breath, Melanie," he said offering a small smile. "There you go," he encouraged when she attempted to obey, "deep breaths."

Mel was taken aback by the switch of attitude. That was the first smile Jake had ever offered her. He had a lovely smile, she thought, the thought distracting her for a split second and making her a bit more confident. Seems she wouldn't be dying today. She let out a breath, reminding herself not to be too comfortable yet. She might still be in danger, all she knew.

"I'm going to untie you now, and we are going to have a civil conversation," Jake continued. "Is that okay?" he asked.

Mel nodded, not trusting her voice just yet. Jake untied her swiftly, freeing her. Mel massaged her wrist, pouting at him in complaint of how tight his knots had been. She remained in the chair, emboldened by his uncharacteristic niceness.

"I'm sorry I invaded your privacy, Jake, but I think we'll both agree that topic is far from the most important in this room currently."

Jake nodded his agreement, offering a light chuckle. He was doing everything he could to keep her calm, make her comfortable. He didn't blame her for entering, he blamed himself for not locking up.

"What the hell did I see, Jake?" she blurted. "What are you?"

"What do you think?" Jake returned the question softly. Mel let out a breath. Aliens didn't exist. Any four-year-old knew that. The only people who believed in the existence of UFOs and Area 59 were nutjobs nobody took seriously. She wasn't about to say the word “alien” out loud and gain permanent citizenship into Nutjob Republic.

"You tell me, Jake," Mel said impatiently, hating the position she was being put in.

"All right all right," Jake said, raising both hands in surrender. "I'll tell you what your mind already knows but you’re yet to accept." iIn the silence that followed, Mel hated Jake just a little bit. If he thought this was the time for suspense.

"I am not of this planet. I do not belong on Earth," he stated casually with the ease of a waiter reading off a menu. In reality, Jake's heart was pounding. So much was at stake and hinged in how he handled this situation.

"You're an alien?" Mel whispered, almost afraid to say the words.

"If that's the term you choose to use, yes, I am an alien. My home is called Kathur, in Universe 399."

Mel's head was spinning. She stood up and started pacing from one end of the room to the other. Jake let her pace, discovering during his stay on this planet that humans handled issues differently. Where people from his home would sit still and brainstorm until a solution was found or a resolution come to, humans would exhibit various forms of physical gestures and movements. Coping mechanisms, they called it. Fascinating stuff.

Suddenly she stopped pacing, turning around to face Jake. "Tell me everything," she commanded. "Leave nothing out." Jake brows rose in surprise at her tone, but he chose to simply go along with the flow. He released a deep breath and started.

"I am Jakyne, son of Hadith and servant of Kathur."

"No, servant isn't what you're thinking," he responded, noticing her confused look. "I assure you I am as free as you are. I am a Level 12 member of a respected group of scientists called The Bakri. In this world, they are called anthropologists. The difference is, The Bakri deals with alien civilizations only. Yeah, we call you aliens too," he said, grinning. Mel was too shocked to smile back.

"Sixty of us were sent on missions to sixty planets." Mel's eyes were like saucers at this point. "Yes, Melanie," he responded, reading her thoughts, "there are more planets than you could ever imagine. We are just a tiny speck among other millions of tiny specks. Our mission is simple: gather as much information about the people, their cultures, alien biology, societies and behaviors, past and present."

"What do you hope to do with this information?" Mel asked suspiciously.

"Strictly for educational purposes, I assure you. We are a highly knowledgeable species, one that is always hungry for more knowledge. Learn, learn, learn is all we do. Your planet isn't under any threat, Mel. If anything, you should be worried about your own kind. My projections for humans aren't great."

Mel thought about this for a minute and shrugged, thinking he had to be right. Man seemed to be man's greatest enemy. There was always one rumor of war or another.

"Duration of the mission is sixty months," Jake continued. "Five years," he adjusted, chuckling as Mel glared at him. She was starting to fall for those chuckles of his. She had never seen him so expressive and her attraction for him tripled in the spot. She dragged her attention back to what he was saying, reminding herself how they had gotten here in the first place.

"How long have you got left?" she asked, fascinated and genuinely curious.

"I leave in five months," he responded, marveling at how well she was taking all of this. Was she in denial? He had learned the human mind was able to suppress whatever it deemed too intense for the host. Another fascinating fact he had learned. Was there going to be a delayed explosive reaction to all of this? He hoped not. Jake watched her face fall at his proclamation and wondered why. There certainly was no reason why she would want him around.

"Now, I have a few questions of my own," Jake said, startling her. She remembered she had been caught snooping around his house and grimaced.

"I would ask why you invaded my property, but I think that question answers itself." Mel frowned at him, confused. If not that, what else could he possibly wish to ask her?

"You're always watching me. Why?" Mel's mouth dropped in shock. Before she could say anything, he carried on. "You watch me when I drive out. You watch me in the middle of the night when I watch the sky. Somehow, you're always there whenever I step out. I know it is no coincidence. I'd like to know why."

Mel was mortified. She couldn't remember ever being this embarrassed. "I answered all your questions," he pressed," It's only fair you answer mine."

She cleared her throat. He was right. Considering the weight of information he had just shared with her, she decided Jake deserved the truth. What could it hurt anyway? "The truth, Jake, is I've wanted you since the day I first saw you." Mel was never shy, but with this man, she found herself struggling, her just-do-it nature deserting her. Doggedly, she pushed on. "I have lusted after you for so long and the things I have done to you in my head are so exquisitely delicious, I swore I would bring them to reality. Your aloofness only served to make me burn hotter."

As she spoke, she noticed Jake stare at her with such raw hunger that her mouth went dry. He had never looked at her that way before. She locked her lips and pushed in, determined to finish." I just had to know who you were, what you were about. The curiosity burned me up." She whispered that last part, eyes to the floor. Jake cleared his throat and she looked up, noticing that hungry gaze again. She knew that look. He wanted her. Her heart leapt for joy.

"And now? Now you know what I am?"

Mel thought about it and discovered she didn't care. In fact, she wanted him a million times more now. "Nothing's changed. I still want you," she stated boldly.

"I've got bad news, Mel," he started sadly. " You and I can't be intimate. We aren't of the same specie."

"But..." she started to protest.

"This human skin is merely a shell, Melanie," he cut in. "It is impossible."

Mel nodded, accepting but devastated. She felt like she had lost a loved one.

"You know I can't let you go until I leave your planet, right?" he asks gently. "You will have your freedom, but for security reasons, you have to be in my sights at all times."

Mel nodded, not caring. What difference did it make anyway?

Chapter 5

Mel stared at the green block of food on a white plate before her. If she hadn't just been let in on Jake's secret, she would have sworn it was jelly. On second thought, she reasoned, it looked like a piece of green cake. She was a mix of excitement and nervousness. She was about to try her first alien meal. She giggled, fumbling with the fork in her left hand slightly.

Jake had been watching her keenly. He wouldn't admit it, but he really wanted her to like the first taste she had of something from his home planet. He could not exactly explain why, but somehow, this woman's opinion was starting to become very important to him.

"Why are you laughing?" he inquired.

Mel chuckled again, rushing to explain lest he took offense. "I was just thinking how I am about to have my first alien food, when, a few hours ago, I didn't even think such things exist." She shook her head. "It still feels like some strange, yet exciting dream."

Jake smiled, understanding. Well, not exactly understanding since he was yet to taste earth food. He wondered if he should open up to her about this. He decided not yet, certain she would make him try some as well.

Mel cut a small piece of the food with her fork, noting how it broke apart like a sponge cake. Lifting it to her nose, she snuffed it first. It smelled like nothing she knew and her distrust arose again. "I'm not going to become one of you, right? This isn't some ancient initiation ritual?"

Chuckling, Jake took the fork from her, moving it toward her shut mouth. "Ah," he encouraged. As the food entered Mel's mouth, she was astonished at the texture of the meal. It scattered apart delightfully in her mouth, treating her taste buds to an explosion of strange, yet splendid flavors.

"It is... crumbly," Mel started, confused, but trying to describe what she was tasting, "yet creamy and almost earthy at the same time. What's this made of, Jake?" she asked, eyes lit up in pleasure.

Jake grinned, feeling victorious and relieved at the same time. She loved it. "It's my home's version of your vegetable salad and salad dressing. I could name all four vegetables in that mix for you, but I doubt you'd remember the names."

Mel was struggling to listen, shoving forkful after forkful of alien goodness into her mouth. She frowned slightly, a thought popping into her mind. "How do you get it into this block shape?"

"Oh that," Jake responded. "I came to Earth with my own cooker." He noted her teasing look and laughed. "You can't blame me. Not exactly keen on alien food."

"Hold on!" Mel ordered. "You've been here five years and NEVER had human food?!"

Jake grimaced. He had hoped to keep that particular detail to himself. "Your food seems... scattered. All our meals are cooked and shaped into a block like you're eating. Aside from that, I just haven't been able to work up the courage to try."

He saw the look in her eyes and felt the need to beg, "Please don't make me." Mel laughed at the almost puppy look on his face. "I tried yours," she opposed, "seems only fair you try ours, wouldn't you say?"

Jake shrugged, resigned. "All right. Whenever you're ready."

***

Jake ducked, dodging a snowball. *That was close. That little woman had an arm on her*, he thought, realizing this was his third close shave. He looked at his jacket, white with snow, and shook his head, trying to dislodge the snow he could still feel in his ear.

Mel was feeling good, having more fun than she had had in years. She had hit him twice, and but for his lightning-quick reflexes, it would be four. She looked around the tree she was hiding behind, startled when she realized he had vanished out of sight. She scanned the row of thin trees, certain none was wide enough to completely conceal his tall frame. He was there just a few seconds ago, where could he have vanished to and how had he done it so fast?

"Psst!" Mel turned sharply, astonished he had crept behind her. Before she could move a muscle, a ball of snow smacked her in the face. She screamed, shocked at the icy coldness. She was temporarily blinded and as she wiped the snow off her face, she could hear her attacker chuckle. As her eyes cleared, she realized Jake had another ball of snow ready to be flung at her again.

"Oh, hell no!" she screamed, lunging herself at him. Jake was shocked at how quickly she had moved. He couldn't believe how quickly his back had ended up on the snow. She was above him, pounding on his chest and laughing. "You scoundrel!" she screamed, laughing hysterically, "That got in my eyes!"

Jake caught and held her hands, stalling her gloved assault on his chest. He grinned at her. "You're one to talk. You hit me twice!"

The laughter died down and suddenly, the air around them was charged with electricity. Their heaving chests rose and fell in unison, not as a result of physical exercise this time, but borne of intense awareness of each other and arousal. Their want for each other was apparent and in the icy coldness of snow, their bodies heated up in anticipation.

"You are one heck of a woman," Jake said in a breathy tone, looking deep into her eyes. The feeling wasn't strange to him, as his people shared some emotions with the human race as well, but its manifestations in this human body were a revelation to him. His pulse was racing and he could scarcely breathe. It felt like he would die if she didn't touch him.

As Mel lowered her head and their lips met, just a brief brush of lips. Jake decided that, though it was all strange to him, this side of his human experience was one he certainly liked.

***

Jake stared at the meal before him. It was not strange to him. He had seen people eat it on his expeditions to restaurants he had gone to study human behavior. Of Italian descent, the spaghetti was a worldwide favorite. Never did he think it would be his turn to put the greasy stuff in his mouth. It smelled good, he would give her that, the garlic flavor reminding him of one of his favorite spices back home.

Mel burst out laughing. He had watched Jake for quite some time, entertained by the passing of several expressions on his handsome face. The anxious look on this man's face who, up until the day she entered his home, had hardly shown any emotion, was too much for her to bear. All of his bravado had fled and what was left was resembled a little boy unsure of himself. Mimicking his earlier actions, she took his fork, twirling it and gathering a tiny portion of spaghetti bolognese. Taking a deep breath, Jake opened his mouth. His taste buds are assaulted by something new and exotic and his eyes widened in shock, amazed at how good it was.

Mel chuckled, watching his reaction. The surprised joy on his face eliminated the need to ask him if he liked it. She broke a piece of banana bread she had on the side. Imitating him again, she prompted him to open his mouth. "Ah..."

Jake glared at her, knowing he was being mocked. This elicited another round of laughter from Mel. Her laughter was contagious and he found himself smiling as he opened his mouth, receiving her offering. His brows rose even higher this time, his mind blown from what he tasted. Is this what he had stayed away from for over 4 years? Gently pushing her hand away, Jake dug into his meal, almost forgetting Mel was there.

Mel laughed and moved to the side. She should have figured he was a foodie. Why else would he travel a million miles to another galaxy with his own cooker? Resting on his kitchen counter, she watched him eat to his fill. At intervals, he would look up at her, shake his head, grin and dig back in. She looked at him affectionately and decided in her heart that, though this man—or whatever he was—would be leaving her soon, she would enjoy every minute by his side up until his very last day.

Chapter 6

Mel stared at her “warden” as she had nicknamed him, sleeping on his couch. She was anything but captive, she admitted to herself. They had been together ninety percent of the time for three straight weeks. The snow was starting to let up, but it was still a very chilly January as it always was in Grand Rapids, temperatures dropping as low as 14 degrees at some point. Mel smiled to herself; she had not felt much of the cold being snuggled up to this man practically all the time. They had discovered that they were both cuddle monsters, holding on to each other for hours on end and not letting go. This turned out to be a bittersweet combination of pleasure and pain for Mel. Pleasure at being able to hold this being that had become a very important part of her whenever she wanted and pain because the intimacy could go no further.

Mel ached for Jake and was frustrated to no end that they couldn't get intimate. She had kissed him several times, exploring the sweet taste of his mouth and exploring his body with her hands. However, she had gone no further, recalling what he had said to her that first day. They were different species and couldn't mate. Mel had her moments of doubt. She had felt his response to her after all. But she dared not question his assertion. She was not the expert in the study of alien species after all. He was. What could she possibly know that he didn't? Still, she wondered.

For over three weeks, Mel had been allowed to visit her home only twice. The first time to get the meal she first made him and the second time to empty her fridge and get some clothes. She was not exactly a prisoner, but Jake had been clear on his stand. He was not going to risk her exposing who he was and sabotaging his mission in the process. He was too close to risk it. *Too close indeed,* Mel thought sadly, looking up at his calendar where January 31st had been circled in red. Jake's departure day. The most exciting man she had ever been with was leaving her for good in twenty-four hours and there was nothing she could do about it. She had watched him in fascination as he worked in his secret room day after day, compiling results frantically and storing data. A few hours ago, he had walked into the living room where she warmed herself by the fireplace, a tired smile on his face. "Just confirmed pickup from my Retrieval Unit," he had announced. "I will be picked up at exactly, 2200 hours. 10 o'clock in the night," he adjusted, chuckling as he remembered her dislike of the use of his complex statements.

Mel had nodded stiffly, returning to stare at the bright orange of the fire blankly. Pretending to be happy at this point was an impossible task.

As Mel watched him nap, she decided she had to be with this man in the biblical sense and was going to regret it the rest of her life if she didn't at least try. She started to walk toward him when a thought stopped her in her tracks. She was probably going to have just one shot at this. She had to do it right. For both of them.

Mel changed direction and headed to the guest bedroom which he had given for her use. She opened the closet, took out her small box, and unzipped it. There it was, her trusty nightwear. It was a tiny black number with tiny spaghetti straps and a low-cut bodice. It stopped mid-thigh and was transparent, barely concealing anything, and that was exactly what Mel needed on this particular mission. Looking at her reflection in the mirror, she grinned, confident no man would be able to resist her in this state.

Not even the not-so-human Jake downstairs. If this didn't get his cock up, she would finally accept it was impossible.

As she touched up her hair and face, she heard a voice behind her. "Mel?"

She turned, momentarily startled. She would never get used to how quietly he moved. "Don't sneak up on me," she admonished playfully. She returned to her business with the mirror, standing at an angle where she would be able to see the man behind her; the literal object of all her desires. She tried to play it cool, but her heart was pounding, threatening to escape her chest and, as she combed her full, brown hair, her hands shook.

"Here, let me help with that," Jake said, covering the distance between them in two long strides. She relinquished the comb and watched in the mirror as he started to comb her hair. She struggled for control, the gesture eliciting feelings in her she had never felt and his gentleness was almost her undoing. Abruptly he put down the comb on the dresser and stalked away.

Confused, Mel watched his retreating frame. Worried, she rushed downstairs. Jake was sitting bolt upright on the sofa, eyes fixed on the far wall and a severe frown on his face. Mel rushed to him, squatting and holding his face in her palms. "Jake?" she inquired, "What's wrong?"

Jake shook his head, refusing to speak. Mel, studied him, trying to figure out if she had somehow offended him. Even with the fierce scowl on his face, Jake was easily the most handsome man she had ever seen or known. Her eyes traveled downward and discovered what he was trying to hide—a huge bulge in his crotch area, straining against his sweatpants, begging for release. Her mouth went dry, noting the size his size. Ah. So *that* was the problem.

"Jake," she called, trapping his head with her palms and ensuring she had his full attention. Slowly, his eyes met hers and she realized he was mortified. Mortified because he was feeling something he was forbidden to act on.

"Let me take care of you," she whispered, looking deeply into his eyes. He merely nodded, unable to speak. Jake made no protest as she took his hand and led him up to his bedroom. She wanted him to be as comfortable as possible. She made him sit in the bed and squatted before him, kissing his lips as she helped him take off his tee-shirt and tasting the delicious nectar that could only be Jake's. Mel took her time, kissing his neck, his chest, and hearing his breath catch as a nipple entered her mouth, she proceeded to suck on it. Jake groaned, amazed at what was happening to him and astounded he was capable of experiencing this in this body. He couldn't stop staring at this stunning woman as she moved even lower, kissing every inch of his body. As she pulled his sweatpants down slowly, he marveled at how that singular act alone was so erotic.

His cock popped out, hard and straight. She marveled at the sight, reaching out immediately to stroke his throbbing length. It was hard and had a thick vein running through its center which made Mel shudder involuntarily. As Mel stroked his silky length, she looked into his eyes and noticed they were glazed over. Precum dotted the opening of the glorious cock, and Mel couldn't stop herself from leaning down to lick it off.

The feel of Mel's tongue on his penis gave Jake a jolt so strong he lifted off the bed temporarily in shock. His eyes were wide as saucers and Mel decided she would give him a treat he would never forget. She lowered her mouth to his manhood, opening up and taking the head into her mouth.

She sucked softly, licking the tip and enjoying watching Jake squirm. She took him even deeper, feeling his length in her throat and contracting the muscles, almost sending Jake over the edge. He was long, so there was still enough left for Mel to wrap her hand around and as she sucked him, she stroked him as well. The combination was too much for Jake and a minute later, he could hear a male voice groaning wildly in pleasure. A few moments later, he floated back to earth and realized with wonder, that the male voice belonged to him. The pleasure had been so intense that he had thought for a moment he would pass out.

As he looked down at the woman beneath him, he met a smiling face covered with thick cream and realized with horror that he had deposited his seed on Mel's face. He is about to apologize when Mel puts a finger to his lips. "Shush," she commanded, "We aren't done." Mel walked into the bathroom, got wipes, cleaned her face, and grinned at herself in the mirror. That man had no idea what was about to happen to him tonight.

She returned to a pleasant surprise. Jake was hard and fully erect again. "Oh, good," she purred, walking slowly to Jake. Without ceremony, Mel settled in his lap facing him, and as she lowered her lips to meet his, she guided his length into her. She gasped as he entered her. She felt his girth, touching all parts of her inside, and groaned in pleasure as moved her hips, getting more of his cock. Mel pushed him down until he was lying on his back and went to work, bouncing up and down with reckless abandon.

Jake watched her with fascination, and, for the first time, questioned his decision to go back. He couldn't believe he was mating with a human female. As she seemed to near her climax, he was grateful it was the fiery Mel with whom he shared this moment. Suddenly, Mel screamed, shaking violently. The rapid contraction of her vagina walls around him almost sent him over the edge, but he held on, determined he had a few things he needed to try himself. After a few seconds of shaking and screaming, Mel collapsed on Jake, his manhood still inside her. He stroke her back, murmuring sweet encouragements in his native Kathur tongue and eliciting a few more shakes from Mel.

Jake deftly turned her around, flipping her on her back and copying what she had done earlier. He kissed her all over but was impatient. He wanted her now. As he slid into her slowly, Mel lost all sense of time and location. She scratched his back, not caring if it drew blood, and choked out his name. "Jake..."

He looked down at her and grinned. "My turn."

***

Mel woke up, her body warm and thoroughly satiated. She looked around for her warden but discovered he wasn't in the room with her. She donned the nightgown that had triggered one of the best times of her life and went downstairs, seeking the man that made her grin like an idiot. Mel searched all around the house, calling out to Jake, but got no response. With sudden panic, she remembered that this was his departure day. She ran in to the secret room, pulling the lever and watching the door cave in as usual. In his well-worn armchair, Jake was seated looking at the blank screen of the one alien computer he was yet to unhook.

"Jake," Mel called, approaching him carefully. "What's the matter?"

Jake did not respond. He did not move. He didn't even seem to be breathing. Mel, now panicked, rushed to him, holding his face in her palms as was becoming her custom.

"What's the matter, Jake?" she pleaded. "Please talk to me."

Jake raised bloodshot eyes to meet hers and in them, she could see the anguish. In a choked voice, he responded. "I am unable to transform."

Mel was confused, then slowly, it dawned on her. She stammered not knowing what questions to ask. He resumed speaking, saving her the trouble. "I made love to you in my human form, something I should not have done and now, I can't transform to my true self. I have tried all morning."

"I can't return home in this body. I can never return to my home!" As Jake finished his anguished statement, he bowed his head and began to cry. Quiet, gut-wrenching sobs that shook his entire body and broke Mel's heart.

Mel held him as he cried, swaying and feeling more and more connected to this man. This was her mess, and she was going to fix it. He had inadvertently sacrificed his home for her and she was not going to let him regret that decision.

She waited until he was all cried out and raised his face, kissing him and beaming at him. "I promise you," she started, "you won't have a single dull moment on Earth. I'll make you happy and we'll explore all the goodness this world has to offer. You'll see!"

As Jake hesitated, she kissed him again, deeply this time until she could feel him starting to respond to her. "I have a tiny red dress I've been looking for an excuse to wear. Let's go on a date, so I finally get my excuse." She stood and stretched out her hand, hoping he would take it. Jake stared at the outstretched hand, knowing what taking it meant. It would mean giving up his world, his home. It would signal his acceptance of a new life. Then he looked at the woman whose arm was outstretched and decided it couldn't be that bad. She had made him happier and more excited than he had been all his life. He felt ten years old again. Maybe fifteen.

Smiling, he reached out and took her arm. As she helped pull him up, he swore that, someday, he would find his way back to his home, but until then, he had a date with a smoking hot alien.

THE END

www.ingramcontent.com/pod-product-compliance
Lightning Source LLC
LaVergne TN
LVHW020530160826
845677LV00015B/3992
9798815387324